Geraldine Kaye

Tim and the Red Indian Headdress

Illustrated by Carolyn Dinan

CHILDRENS PRESS, CHICAGO

Library of Congress Cataloging in Publication Data

Kaye, Geraldine.
  Tim and the Red Indian headdress.

  SUMMARY: To please his little sister, Tim makes
her an Indian headdress like his own.
    [1.   Brothers and sisters—Fiction]   I.   Dinan,
Carolyn.   II.   Title.
PZ7.K212Ti4   [E]   75-41377
ISBN 0-516-03594-0

American edition published 1976 by
Regensteiner Publishing Enterprises, Inc.
All rights reserved. Printed in the U.S.A.
Published simultaneously in Canada.

First published 1973 by Knight books and
Brockhampton Press Ltd, Salisbury Road, Leicester
Printed in Great Britain by Cox & Wyman Ltd,
London, Fakenham and Reading
Second impression 1974
Text copyright © 1973 Geraldine Kaye
Illustrations copyright © 1973 Brockhampton Press Ltd

Mom was sewing some new curtains.

"Can I do it?" Tim said.

"Me," said Betsy.

"I'd better do it myself," said Mom.

Tim sat on the floor. He put some tape on his arm like a bandage.

"Look at my bandage," Tim said.

"Me," said Betsy.

There was a knock at the door.

"Postman," said Tim.

The postman held out a brown paper parcel.

"It's from Granny," said Mom.

"Me, me," said Betsy.

"No, let Tim undo it," said Mom.

Tim undid the string with his teeth.
Inside the brown paper was a Red Indian
headdress.

"Me, me," said Betsy.

"No, it's for Tim," said Mom.

"Look at these feathers," said Tim.
"I bet somebody went all round the world
getting them."

Tim put the headdress on.

"Me, me," said Betsy.

"This is for Betsy," said Mom. It was a dress with little pink roses. "Look, Betsy, isn't it pretty?" Mom said.

"Betsy want hat," said Betsy. She was going to cry.

Mom put the dress over Betsy's head.
"Hat?" said Betsy.

But the dress wouldn't go on. It was too small.

"Oh dear," said Mom. "Betsy is a big girl now."

"Hat," screamed Betsy.

Tim went out to the Browns' farm.

"Baa," said the sheep.

Tim wasn't frightened of sheep. "Baa," said Tim.

15

Rover was asleep in the yard. Tim walked past on tiptoe.

"Not frightened of the old dog, are you?" said Mr. Brown.

"May I have some feathers?" Tim said.

"Help yourself," said Mr. Brown.

Tim went to the barn. There were feathers all over the floor. Tim picked them up.

"Good-bye, Mr. Brown," Tim said.
"Good-bye, Rover."
Tim walked back across the field.
"Baa," said the sheep.
"Baa," said Tim.

Tim went into his back garden.

He put his feathers on the grass.

Then he got his paint box.

"What are you doing?" Mom called.

"Something with paint," said Tim. He was painting feathers.

"Me," said Betsy.

"Dinner," said Mom.

"All right," said Tim. He put the feathers on the grass to dry.

After dinner Tim went out into the
garden. He took the tape off his arm. He
put the feathers on it.

"What are you doing, Mom?" Tim called.

"Something with sticks," said Mom.

"This is a small Red Indian headdress for Betsy," said Tim.

"What's that?" said Tim.

"It's a Red Indian wigwam for you," said Mom.

"I'll make a small one for Betsy," said Tim. And so he did.